Beneath the *Poinciana Sky*

A Coming of Age Novel

KAYANNA J. WILLIAMS

EDITED BY
KABRENA L. ROBINSON

Beneath the Poinciana Sky

Copyright © 2025 by Kayanna J. Williams
All rights reserved.

No part of this publication may be reproduced, distributed, or transmitted in any form or by any means, including photocopying, recording, or other electronic or mechanical methods, without the prior written permission of the copyright holder, except as permitted by copyright law.

First Edition 2025

ISBN:
Hardcover: 978-1-998245-49-9
Paperback: 978-1-998245-48-2

Cover and book design by Kabrena L. Robinson
Published by Eva-Michelle & Family Publishing
www.evamichelleandfamily.com

For the girls who feel like outsiders in a world

that asks them to shrink—

The dreamers, the quiet ones, the brave hearts

who love deeply but doubt their place.

This is for you.

A reminder that you are not too much.

You are meant to take up space, to speak your

truth, to shine.

May this story light the path toward your

becoming.

Contents

Introduction

Some people are born ready to take up space. I was not one of those people.

For as long as I can remember, I tried to shrink myself—to fold into corners, to blend in so seamlessly that no one would notice me. Not because I didn't want to be seen, but because being seen often came with expectations I wasn't sure I could meet. Being seen meant people would have opinions, judgements, and sometimes even ridicule. And for a girl like me, growing up in a small town where everybody knew everybody, the last thing I wanted was to be the centre of attention.

But the funny thing about trying to disappear is that life has a way of forcing you into the light, whether you're ready or not.

I am Jasmine Sinclair—an 18-year-old girl standing at the

crossroads of her past and her future. Tall, slim, with deep chocolate-brown skin, thick hair that seems to have a mind of its own, and brown eyes that have seen the world in shades of doubt and hope, fear and resilience. I have spent years figuring out who I am, and I am still learning. But one thing I know for sure: I am done hiding.

This story is about love.

Not just the kind of love that makes your heart race and your breath catch, but the kind of love that is even harder to find—the love for yourself.

For years, I questioned whether I was enough. I worried that my voice was too small, that my dreams were too big, that the things I wanted—to write, to love freely, to exist unapologetically—were things I wasn't allowed to have.

This is for the girls who feel like they don't belong.

For the ones who have ever doubted their beauty, their intelligence, their worth.

For the quiet ones who have words locked inside them, waiting for the day they feel brave enough to speak.

For the ones who love differently, and for the ones who don't know yet who they are meant to love.

For every girl who has been told to be less—less loud, less opinionated, less ambitious, less herself.

This is your reminder that you do not have to shrink to make others comfortable.

You are allowed to take up space. You are allowed to want things. You are allowed to be seen.

This is the story of how everything changed.

Of how I stopped running.

Of how I finally chose me.

And if you're reading this, maybe it's time for you to choose yourself too.

CHAPTER 1

The Unforgettable Crush

The sun blazed overhead, its golden rays bouncing off the pavement as the scent of new possibilities mixed with the familiar warmth of my island home. The first day of school after a long summer always carried a certain buzz—a crackling energy of fresh starts and familiar faces.

I adjusted the strap of my bag, trying to steady the nerves twisting in my stomach. Another year. Another attempt to navigate the unspoken rules of prep school. I had always been the girl who blended into the background—too quiet, too unsure, too caught up in my own thoughts.

And then, I heard his voice.

"Jasmine, right?"

I turned, startled, my heart skipping an embarrassing beat. And that was the first time I saw him.

Elliott.

There was something about him—something that made the air around him feel charged. He was a couple of months older than me, taller, with piercing brown eyes and messy black hair that looked like he had just rolled out of bed but somehow made it work. He had an effortless charm, a kind of natural magnetism that made people want to be close to him. Unlike me—awkward, unsure, never quite knowing how to take up space—he moved through the world like he belonged everywhere.

I was immediately smitten.

From that moment on, Elliott and I became inseparable. We spent our days playing pranks on each other, passing notes in class and sharing secrets under the old guinep tree behind the cafeteria. He was the one person who made me feel like I could just *be*—without expectations, without fear of saying the wrong thing.

And yet, despite my growing feelings, I never told him the truth. I convinced myself that he didn't see me that way.

Then, we went to different high schools, and just like that —he was gone. No dramatic goodbye, no promises to keep in touch. Just the quiet ache of knowing that someone who once felt like home had become a stranger.

Fast forward to now.

Sixth form after high school was supposed to be a fresh start. A chance to step out of the shy, awkward shadow of my younger self. I had my best friends—Elle, Anna, and Kayla—and together, we were finally living the teenage dream. Late-night adventures. Beach days. Music blasting from car speakers as we drove with the windows down. Life felt wide open.

Until that night.

The prep school reunion was held at a hilltop villa overlooking the sea. The sky was streaked with pink and orange, the scent of jerk chicken and fresh coconut wafting through the air. Music pulsed through the speakers, blending with the sound of laughter and old friends catching up.

I wasn't thinking about Elliott. Not until I saw him.

It was like the world tilted for a second. Same piercing brown eyes. Same messy black hair.

But he wasn't the same boy I remembered.

He was taller now, broader, with a confidence that had settled into him like second nature. His voice was deeper, smoother—the kind of voice that could make anyone stop and listen.

I barely had time to process my emotions before our eyes met across the crowd. A flicker of recognition flashed across his face, followed by something else—something unreadable.

"Jasmine?" he said, stepping closer.

I forced a smile, hoping my voice wouldn't betray the pounding of my heart. "Elliott."

We exchanged polite hellos—the kind people give when they're unsure whether they're supposed to remember each other. But I remembered everything.

The conversation was cautious, careful. Small talk about

school, life, how different everything felt now. He was doing sixth form at my school now—something I hadn't even known.

Then, the night ended, and I walked away, telling myself it was just another fleeting moment.

But then, a message.

Out of nowhere, Elliott slid into my DMs on Instagram.

"Hey. It was really good seeing you tonight."

I stared at my phone for way too long, debating how to respond. And then, I did.

"Yeah, it was. Crazy how time flies."

That was the beginning.

It started off simple—casual check-ins, catching up on lost years. But before I knew it, we were talking every day. About school. Our plans for the future. The things we never said. The way he typed felt familiar—like slipping into an old rhythm I thought I had forgotten.

And then he asked the question that stopped me in my tracks.

"How did we even get here?"

I stared at the screen, fingers hovering over the keyboard. How had I let it get this far?

I took three hours to respond, overthinking every word, every punctuation mark, every possible outcome.

What if I misread everything? What if he only saw me as a childhood friend?

But when I finally replied, his answer made my heart stop. "I've been thinking about you."

And now?

Here I am—eighteen years old, juggling a part-time job at the local stationery store with my dreams of becoming a writer. My life is filled with laughter, good friends, and the gentle hum of my small-town island life.

But every night, it always comes back to him.

Elliott and I text every day—about everything and nothing. He tells me I'm beautiful. He says he admires my strength, my independence, my drive.

And I believe him.

Most of the time.

But here's the thing.

Despite all this verbal affection, he's never asked me out on a real date. Never planned a walk on the beach. Never suggested grabbing ice cream at our favourite shop. It's as if we're caught in a loop of *almosts* and unspoken possibilities.

And I can't tell if he's afraid—

Or if I'm just one of many girls he whispers sweet words to in the dark.

The uncertainty burns.

Every time my phone lights up with his name, my heart leaps, only to crash when the conversation never crosses that invisible line.

So, what am I to him?

A childhood memory?

A passing distraction?

Or something more?

There are moments when I catch him looking at me—his

gaze lingering just a second too long, like he's searching for something.

Moments when he types, pauses, then deletes—like he wants to say something real, but stops himself.

Moments when I think he wants this just as much as I do.

But he never says it.

And I never ask.

Because deep down, I'm scared.

Scared that if I push, I'll break the fragile thread holding us together.

Scared that if I reach for more, I'll find nothing.

But I can't keep living in uncertainty.

So, I ask myself the question that keeps me up at night: *Will Elliott ever take a chance on us? Or am I just another what-if?*

CHAPTER 2

The Ghost of My Past

I thought I had closure with Nic.

She was my first love, my first heartbreak, my first real lesson in betrayal. What we had was never easy, never simple —hiding in the shadows, whispering in the halls, stealing moments behind locked doors. On an island where tradition ran deep and expectations were heavy, love like ours had to be kept quiet.

And then she shattered it.

Just days before graduation, I found out she cheated on me—with a guy, no less. It was like a punch to the gut, leaving me breathless and questioning everything. But I had healed. Or so I thought.

Then she messaged me.

Nic: Jas, I know I'm the last person you want to hear from, but please. Can we talk? I need to make things right.

I stared at the screen, my heart pounding. Every part of me screamed to ignore it—to leave her in the past where she belonged. But curiosity was a dangerous thing.

So I replied.

Me: What's there to talk about?

Her response came instantly.

Nic: I never got to explain. I owe you that much.

I hesitated before typing:

Me: A phone call. That's all I can give you.

Nic: I'll take it.

Later that night, I paced my room, my fingers trembling as I finally hit the call button.

"Jasmine," Nic breathed as she answered. Hearing her voice sent a shiver through me, dragging old emotions to the surface.

"Talk," I said flatly, keeping my guard up.

She exhaled sharply. "I messed up. I was a coward. I let the pressure of everything get to me, and I hurt you in the worst way. And I'm sorry, Jas. I really, really am."

I clenched my jaw. "You didn't just hurt me, Nic. You made me feel like I wasn't enough."

Her voice wavered. "I was scared. You know what it was like for us, always looking over our shoulders. I thought maybe... if I could just be 'normal,' everything would be easier."

"Did it work?" I challenged.

Silence.

Finally, she whispered, "No. It just made me realise what I lost."

"Goodbye, Nic."

"Goodbye, Jasmine."

It was unlike me to be this cold, but the wound from that relationship was still fresh. I ended the call, my heart pounding.

But something still didn't feel finished.

The weight of that conversation stayed with me.

What troubled me more was the fear of telling Elliott about Nic. What would he think if he knew I had once given my heart to another girl? Would he still want me, knowing the secrets I carried?

Deep down, I knew I didn't want to be with Nic anymore. I craved the genuine connection I shared with Elliott—a love that was honest and open. Yet, the fear of rejection and judgement held me back. Torn between moving on and clinging to echoes of my past, I realised one thing: I had to be true to myself and to Elliott if I ever hoped to move forward.

Days turned into weeks, and every time Elliott's name lit up my phone, my heart pounded with both anticipation and dread. On sunlit afternoons, as we exchanged jokes and memes, I longed to reveal every facet of my life—especially the complicated chapter with Nic. But with every message, guilt crashed over me like a tidal wave.

One evening, as we chatted about an upcoming concert,

he casually asked about my "love life."

"So, any past flames I should be jealous of?" he teased, his voice light yet probing.

I forced a laugh. "Oh, you know, just me being me." Elliott chuckled. "Mysterious as always." After a pause, he added, "You can tell me, you know. I'd never judge you."

My heart raced. Could he see through my carefully guarded secrets?

"It's complicated," I admitted, running a hand through my hair. "But maybe... maybe I'll tell you soon."

"Soon, huh?" His tone softened. "I'll hold you to that."

His words pressed on me—a silent plea for honesty I couldn't ignore.

After agonizing days of deliberation, I sent a message to Nic, and we agreed to meet up at the familiar café in town. My pulse quickened as I prepared to face the echoes of what once was.

Nic was already seated when I arrived, stirring sugar into her tea. She looked up, her deep bronze skin illuminated by the golden glow of the café lights, dark curls framing her face in soft waves. Her almond-shaped eyes—light brown with flecks of gold—held that familiar intensity, the same quiet fire I once fell for.

"I didn't think you'd come," she admitted.

"Neither did I," I said honestly, sliding into the seat across from her.

For a long moment, neither of us spoke.

Finally, Nic sighed. "I don't expect you to forgive me, Jas.

I just… I needed to see you one last time."

I studied her. The girl I once loved. The girl who broke me.

I took a slow sip, returning my focus to the present, choosing my words with care. "I'm not mad," I said softly. "I just don't understand why you reached out now."

"I've been looking back at everything we had," she continued, "and I realize what I lost. I was selfish and hurtful. I'm sorry for everything."

Her sincerity cut through me, yet the scars remained. "I appreciate that," I replied, though deep inside, I knew it was too late.

She sighed, tracing her finger along the rim of her cup. "Do you ever think about us?"

I met her gaze steadily. "I think about how much I've changed—and how much I don't want to go back to that secret life."

For a moment, the confident Nic I once knew faltered. "I get it," she whispered. "But I still miss you."

I shook my head firmly. "I'm moving forward, Nic. And I think you should too."

A sad smile flickered on her face. "I hope Elliott knows how lucky he is."

I froze. "What do you mean?"

She let out a small laugh, shaking her head. "You think I don't see it? The way you talk about him? You're in deep, Jasmine."

My throat tightened, but I didn't argue. Instead, I stood,

my decision resolute. "Goodbye, Nic."

Walking out into the balmy evening, I inhaled deeply, feeling the weight of the past begin to lift. Yet, as I made my way along the bustling street, the warmth of the night did little to quell the storm inside me. I couldn't shake the mixture of finality and uncertainty that swirled together—a promise that this was not the end, but the beginning of something new.

I dialled Elle's number, needing a familiar voice to steady my racing heart. Over a quick call, she reminded me that honesty was the only way forward and that Elliott had always admired my strength. "You deserve someone who sees all of you, Jasmine," she said, her words igniting a spark of hope within me.

Back in my room, I sat by the open window, letting the soft night breeze brush against my skin, the rhythmic hum of crickets filling the quiet. The world outside felt still, but inside me, everything was shifting.

Tomorrow—maybe even sooner—I would tell Elliott everything. The truth could no longer stay buried beneath fear and uncertainty. No more hiding. No more looking back.

I traced patterns on the windowsill, my fingers unsteady, my heart racing. Nic was my past. Elliott... he could be something more. But only if he wanted to be.

And as I gazed out into the dark, one thought lingered, refusing to fade.

Would Elliott still be there once I finally set myself free?

CHAPTER 3

The Moment of Truth

That night, I found myself staring at my phone, my hands trembling as I drafted a message to Elliott. My heart raced as I let the words flow from my fingers, unsure of how they would be received.

Hey Elliott, I typed. *Can we talk? There's something important I need to share.*

His reply came almost immediately—typical of him.

Of course! I'm here for you. What's up?

My breath caught in my throat. This wasn't just a casual conversation. I was about to reveal a part of my life that had haunted me for months. It's about my past... about Nic.

I swallowed hard, praying for the courage to press send. Would he understand? Would he still want to talk to me afterward?

I hit send. It felt like pulling a thread that could unravel everything between us.

Okay, let's talk about it, he replied quickly. When and where?

We agreed to meet at a local seaside restaurant on Friday evening—a favourite spot for both of us. It was the kind of place where the warm, briny breeze carried the scent of grilled fish and fried plantains, where the soft glow of string lights reflected off the waves. The sound of the tide rolling in blended with the hum of conversation, creating a sense of calm I desperately needed.

Friday arrived with its usual rush, but my mind was a storm. I got there early, hoping to collect myself. The restaurant buzzed with life—the clinking of glasses, the scrape of utensils against plates, bursts of laughter from a nearby table. Yet all I could hear was the pounding of my own heart.

When Elliott finally walked in, he brought with him an effortless warmth that eased my nerves, if only for a moment. His easy stride, the way his eyes lit up when he spotted me—just for a second, it felt like everything might be okay.

He slid into the seat across from me, and before I could gather my thoughts, the waitress appeared. My mind wasn't present, but Elliott didn't hesitate. He glanced at me and, with a soft smile, placed the order for both of us.

"Two cold Tings, rice and peas with oxtail for her, and escovitch fish for me."

It was so natural, so thoughtful—as if he had memorized

the things that brought me comfort. That simple gesture, his quiet understanding, melted a fraction of the tension coiled inside me.

"Thanks for being here," I murmured, my voice unsteady as I met his gaze.

"Of course. You can talk to me about anything," he said gently, leaning in.

Taking a deep breath, I told him everything—my relationship with Nic, the heartbreak, the betrayal, the silence I'd kept for so long. The words came out raw and real, each one peeling back layers I had kept hidden. As I spoke, I watched Elliott's expression shift—from curiosity to concern, then to something softer.

Then I paused. My pulse thundered in my ears as I braced for rejection.

"I didn't know how to tell you," I whispered. "And I understand if you... if you think differently about me now."

Elliott reached across the table, his hand warm over mine. "I appreciate your honesty," he said. "That takes a lot of strength. Your past doesn't change how I feel about you. I just want to know you—and support you."

Relief washed over me like a tide. A weight I hadn't even known I was carrying lifted, letting me breathe again. For the first time, I could imagine a future built on honesty—not fear.

As we continued talking, the tension faded. Elliott listened intently—not just accepting my past, but trying to understand it. His presence, his patience, was more than I ever dared to hope for.

"Can I ask you something?" he said after a while, his brown eyes holding mine.

I nodded.

"Was there ever a part of you that thought about how this would affect us?"

I hesitated. "Honestly? Yes. I was terrified. I didn't want to lose what we have before it had a chance to become something real."

He nodded thoughtfully. "I get that. But we all have histories. Getting to know someone means embracing every part of them. The past doesn't define you—but it helps me understand the person I care about."

His words anchored me. I had spent so long feeling torn between the past and the future, but in this moment, everything felt clearer.

"What about you?" I asked, wanting to know more about the boy who had become my safe space. "What's your story?"

He smirked, leaning back in his seat. "I've had my fair share of awkward crushes," he admitted. "There was this one time..."

He launched into a hilarious story about a failed confession that had us both laughing until our sides hurt. With each laugh, we drew closer—rewriting our story with trust, honesty, and light-heartedness.

Eventually, the night slipped into quiet. As we stepped outside, the warm Caribbean breeze kissed my skin. The rhythmic crash of waves filled the silence as streetlights flickered to life above us.

Elliott rubbed the back of his neck, a hopeful smile tugging at his lips. "I've been meaning to ask you something."

I tilted my head. "What is it?"

He took a step closer. "Would you be my girlfriend?"

I blinked. I had imagined this moment countless times, but never dared to believe it would actually happen.

My smile spread slowly. "Yes. Of course, yes."

His grin grew. "Good. Because I also wanted to ask you on a proper date. Dinner and a movie kind of thing."

Laughter bubbled up from my chest. "I'd love that."

As we stood beneath the glowing streetlights, something shifted. The laughter faded into stillness—one of those moments filled with everything unsaid. I looked up, and he was already watching me.

I stepped forward and kissed him.

It was soft at first, tentative. But the spark was undeniable. A rush of relief and emotion—something that had been quietly building finally breaking free.

When we pulled apart, Elliott's smile mirrored my own.

"Can we do that again?" he asked, teasing but sincere.

"Definitely," I said, the word catching in my throat like a promise.

And just like that, the past loosened its grip. What lay ahead was still uncertain—but for once, it didn't scare me.

I was ready for whatever came next.

CHAPTER 4

Changing Seasons

As the tropical winter season transitioned into spring, I felt myself coming alive in ways I never had before. The poinciana tree on the school grounds had begun to bloom, its fiery red petals scattered across the pavement like nature's own warning sign. It was the first true signal that the seasons were changing, that the slow lull of tropical winter had given way to spring's arrival.

For years, the poinciana had been more than just a symbol of exams creeping closer—it was a backdrop to my life. It was where my friends and I gathered under its shade between classes, where our conversations shifted from schoolwork to dreams of the future. And now, it had become something else entirely. A quiet witness to the unfolding story between Elliott and me.

My romance with Elliott had blossomed alongside the changing seasons, each day bringing a new layer of warmth and excitement. Our connection grew effortlessly—late-night calls filled with laughter, stolen glances in the hallways, the gentle way he reached for my hand as we walked. With him, everything felt like it was falling into place.

But school had a way of reminding me that reality wasn't all daydreams and stolen kisses. Exam season loomed over us, an unavoidable storm before the much-needed summer break. In the middle of all the studying, Elliott suggested we all meet up at our usual weekend hangout—the KFC in town. It was a routine gathering, an unspoken tradition, and I was more than ready for the break.

I arrived a little late, pushing through the heavy doors to find Elle, Anna, and Kayla already seated in our favourite booth. The air buzzed with energy—a mixture of grease, laughter, and the low hum of weekend conversations. Elliott caught my eye immediately, flashing me that lopsided grin that always made my heart stutter. He scooted over, making room for me to slide in beside him, his arm casually draping around my shoulders.

Elle was in the middle of telling a ridiculous story about her failed attempt to make homemade dumplings.

"I swear, they were like actual rocks," she groaned, waving a fry in the air for emphasis.

Anna cackled, nearly choking on her drink. "Did you seriously follow a recipe, or did you just wing it?"

"I watched a YouTube video! I thought it looked easy!" Elle protested, but even she couldn't keep a straight face. Kayla snorted. "Next time, maybe don't get your culinary skills from someone named Chef Boy Wasted."

The laughter rolled through the group, light and carefree. It was the kind of moment I wanted to bottle up, to keep forever. But just as I was settling into the comfort of it, the atmosphere shifted.

The door swung open, and in walked Nic.

A chill rushed through me, the warmth of the evening vanishing in an instant. The sound of the restaurant seemed to fade into the background, my heartbeat suddenly deafening.

She looked different—her posture more reserved, her expression unreadable. But it was her eyes that got me. They were searching, hesitant, as if testing the waters before diving in.

Elle noticed my sudden silence and followed my gaze. "Who's that?" she asked, her voice laced with curiosity.

I swallowed hard, my throat dry. "That's Nic," I said, barely above a whisper.

Elliott straightened beside me, his arm slipping from my shoulders. "The Nic?"

Elle's expression tightened slightly, but she said nothing. She was the only one who knew the full truth—the only one I had ever confided in about Nic and what we had been to each other. Anna and Kayla might have suspected, having seen us together in the past, but I had never confirmed anything to them.

Nic's eyes locked onto mine, and for a moment, the world around us disappeared. Then she took a step forward.

"Can we talk?" she asked, her voice quieter than I expected.

The table fell silent. The easy energy from earlier was gone, replaced by an unspoken tension that pressed against my chest.

Elle glanced at me, then at Nic, her eyes narrowing slightly. "Is everything okay?"

I couldn't answer. I didn't know. I wasn't ready for this —wasn't ready to unravel the past in front of the people who had become my safe space. But Nic had a way of forcing confrontation, even without meaning to.

Elliott cleared his throat, shifting uncomfortably. "Look, if you two need a minute, we can—"

"No." I cut in, shaking my head. "Not here. Not now."

Nic's shoulders sagged slightly, but she nodded. "Okay. Just... let me know when you're ready."

With that, she turned and walked away, disappearing through the doors as quickly as she had entered.

A heavy silence lingered in her wake.
Elle was the first to speak. "Okay, what the hell was that?"

I let out a slow breath, trying to gather myself. "It's complicated."

Anna exchanged a glance with Kayla, who shrugged. "Isn't it always?" Kayla said, but there was no malice in her tone—only understanding.

Elliott reached for my hand, giving it a gentle squeeze. "You don't have to explain anything you're not ready to."

I met his gaze, gratitude swelling in my chest. But deep down, I knew that ignoring this wouldn't make it go away. Nic's presence had reopened wounds I thought had started to heal, and whether I liked it or not, I needed to confront them.

The rest of the night passed in a blur, but the weight of what had just happened clung to me. By the time I got home, I had already made up my mind.

I texted Nic: *Tomorrow. We'll talk.*

Her response came quickly: *Thank you.*

The following afternoon, I sat on a worn-out bench in the quiet garden behind the library. The spring air carried the scent of fresh blossoms, a sharp contrast to the turmoil brewing inside me. When Nic arrived, she hesitated before sitting beside me, leaving just enough space between us to acknowledge the distance time had placed there.

"Thanks for coming," she said, her voice softer than I remembered.

I nodded, my fingers tracing patterns on my jeans. "Say what you need to say."

She exhaled. "I just... I wanted to apologise. For everything. I know I hurt you, and I've spent a long time trying to understand why."

I swallowed hard, the emotions bubbling beneath the surface. "You can't undo the past, Nic."

"I know." She looked down at her hands, then back up at

me, her expression raw. "But seeing you with Elliott... it stings. You're so open with him, so free. We never had that. We had to hide. And now, you get to live your truth, but only in a way that feels safe."

I stiffened. "What's that supposed to mean?"

Nic shook her head. "I think you're using him as a cover-up. You're afraid to let the world know who you really are."

Her words hit like a punch to the gut. "That's not fair."

"Isn't it?" she challenged. "You're happy with him, I can see that. But are you happy with yourself?"

I had no answer. The truth clawed at me, unravelling parts of me I wasn't ready to face.

Nic stood up, her face unreadable. "I hope one day you can be honest with yourself the way you deserve to be."

And with that, she walked away, leaving me alone with the weight of her words.

That evening, I found myself in Elliott's arms, my head resting against his chest. "I feel like I don't even know who I am," I admitted, my voice barely above a whisper.

Elliott kissed the top of my head gently. "You're brave, Jasmine. But figuring yourself out doesn't have to be on anyone else's timeline but yours."

I squeezed my eyes shut, letting his words sink in. Maybe he was right. Maybe the journey to truth was mine to take—at my own pace, in my own way.

CHAPTER 5

The Backlash

Nic's words echoed relentlessly in my mind, a quiet torment lingering beneath the surface, even as my relationship with Elliott grew stronger. As spring warmed into summer, I found myself becoming more and more immersed in his world—meeting his parents, laughing with his siblings, and being openly introduced as his girlfriend to his tight-knit circle of friends. On the surface, everything seemed perfect. But inside, a restlessness gnawed at the edges of my happiness.

One evening, I lay sprawled across my bed, scrolling aimlessly through Instagram, when my breath caught sharply. A post on a popular local gossip page featured a blurry photo of Elliott and me holding hands. The caption was worse than the image: "Their relationship is fake—there's a secret about who she really is."

My stomach twisted. It had to be Nic. The accusation felt too personal, too specific after our last encounter. Who else would even think to say something like that?

The worry gnawed at me all night, the words from that post echoing in my dreams like distant thunder.

The next morning, I welcomed the distraction of work. Kayla and I shared shifts at a quaint stationery store in town —a haven lined with journals and stacks of books. It had become my safe space, a quiet corner of the world where I could be myself, where my love for writing and literature could breathe. Kayla, with her quick wit and artistic flair, always knew how to lift the heaviness from my shoulders.

During our lunch break, seated in the storeroom surrounded by boxes of school supplies, I finally let go of the secret I had been holding onto.

"Kayla, there's something I need to tell you," I began, fingers fiddling with the edge of my sandwich wrapper.

She looked up from her sketchpad, already sensing the seriousness in my voice. "Is this about that Instagram post?"

I nodded, my throat tightening. "Yeah... but it's more than that. It's about Nic."

Kayla shifted her body to face me fully, her sketchpad forgotten. "Okay. I'm listening."

And so, amidst the scent of paper and ink, I told her everything—about my relationship with Nic, the secrecy, the heartbreak, and the recent confrontation that had left me feeling exposed and conflicted.

Kayla didn't interrupt once. Her eyes stayed on mine,

her expression calm, open, and full of understanding.

When I finally finished, she exhaled slowly. "Wow. Jasmine... thank you for trusting me with that. Seriously."

I blinked, surprised by how much her words meant.

She continued, "Look, no one else gets to define who you are. Not Nic, not that gossip page. You know your truth. And as far as I can see, you're doing just fine."

A warmth rose in my chest, gratitude swelling in a way I hadn't expected. "Thanks, Kayla."

She reached over, giving my hand a gentle squeeze. "Anytime. And just so you know, Elliott's clearly crazy about you. That much is obvious."

I smiled, the tension in my shoulders easing, if only a little.

But the days that followed were difficult. The gossip post had spread like wildfire. Everywhere I went, it felt like people were whispering behind cupped hands, stealing glances as I passed. The judgement in their eyes—real or imagined—felt suffocating.

Elle noticed immediately. After class one afternoon, she pulled me aside, concern written all over her face.

"You know you can't control what people say, right?" she said gently. "You and Elliott—you know what's real. That's what matters."

I nodded, fighting the lump rising in my throat. "I know... it's just hard. It feels like everything I tried to move past is coming back. Like I'm being dragged backward when I've fought so hard to move forward."

She hugged me, holding on a little longer than usual. "You don't owe anyone an explanation, Jasmine. But you do owe yourself peace."

Despite Elle and Kayla's encouragement, I knew what I had to do. Elliott deserved the truth from me—not just about the post, but about how I was really feeling. We made plans to meet that evening at his house, a place that had become unexpectedly familiar over the past few months.

We sat together on his veranda, where the breeze carried the sound of music from a nearby shop, mingled with distant laughter and the clinking of bottles. It should have been comforting, but I felt anything but calm.

"Elliott," I said, my voice shaking, "I need to talk to you about something."

He turned toward me, his expression instantly serious. "What's going on?"

I took a deep breath and told him everything—the Instagram post, my suspicions about Nic, the feelings it stirred in me, the doubts I hadn't dared to say aloud.

He didn't interrupt. He didn't pull away. When I finished, he reached for my hand, steady and sure.

"Jasmine," he said, his voice low, "none of that changes how I feel about you. You're strong, you're honest, and you're real. That's the girl I've fallen for."

I felt the tears rising before I could stop them. But they weren't just tears of pain. They were tears of relief.

Then Elliott pulled out a small velvet box. My breath caught in my throat as he opened it, revealing a delicate promise ring, simple but beautiful.

"This isn't just about what's happening now," he said, gently slipping it onto my finger. "It's a promise. Whatever comes, we face it together. You're not alone in this."

I couldn't speak. I just nodded, tears streaming freely now. And when I leaned into him, everything else faded away.

Later that night, in the quiet of my room, I opened Instagram again and froze.

Nic had posted a photo.

She was smiling, standing against the backdrop of a pink-streaked sky, her arm draped around another girl. The caption was simple: "New beginnings."

A strange mix of emotions surged in me—jealousy, confusion, sadness. Was she really moving on? Was it genuine, or another way to stir me up?

I closed the app, frustration bubbling to the surface. Why did it still affect me? I had Elliott. I had what I wanted... didn't I?

But the truth was messy.

Nic's words still haunted me.

Was I using Elliott as a shield? Was I hiding, even from myself?

I stared at the promise ring on my finger, its silver band glinting softly in the moonlight. No matter how complicated the path forward seemed, I wasn't walking it alone.

And maybe, just maybe, I was ready to face the truth.

CHAPTER 6

Summer Secrets

The relief of my last exam washing away brought a sense of liberation unlike any other. School was finally closing for the summer, promising long days of adventure, freedom, and possibilities. As I stepped out of the exam room, feeling the tension slide off my shoulders, Elliott greeted me with a broad, welcoming grin that instantly filled me with warmth.

"You survived!" he joked, slipping an arm around my shoulders as we walked across the sunlit courtyard.

"Barely," I laughed, feeling genuinely lighter. "But summer is finally ours now."

"And I have a feeling it's going to be unforgettable," he said, pulling me closer.

Over the next few days, the excitement of summer built steadily among our group of friends. Elle, Kayla, Anna, and

Elliott had become my circle—each bringing their unique energy and strength to my life. Anna, always the adventurous one, had offered her family's beach house as a getaway to kickstart the summer. As the wealthiest among us, her family owned several prominent businesses in town, from supermarkets to car dealerships. On our small island, Anna's light skin, long hair, and affluent background made her the most popular girl at school, a popularity tinged with a bitter undercurrent of colourism that the island unfortunately perpetuated. Still, beneath the surface, Anna was kind, generous, and fiercely loyal to those she loved.

We gathered at our usual weekend spot—the local KFC in the bustling town square—to discuss plans over plates of spicy chicken and fries.

"It's going to be epic!" Anna announced excitedly, brushing back her long, flowing hair. "I've already told my parents, and they're totally cool with it. We can leave Friday after work. Everyone in?"

"Obviously," Kayla said with a grin, dipping a fry into ketchup. Her usual reserved nature was brightened by the prospect of a relaxing weekend. Kayla was quiet, but her subtle humour and creative insights had always drawn me to her.

Elle nodded enthusiastically, her infectious laugh filling the table. "I'm ready! Just promise me we won't do any crazy midnight swims."

Elliott leaned back comfortably, his arm casually draped around my chair. "I'm in for whatever. As long as there's food, I'm good."

We all laughed, and for a moment, everything felt perfect. Yet underneath the excitement, a small worry continued to gnaw at me. The recent Instagram drama, Nic's cryptic post, and my growing uncertainties still lingered beneath my joy.

The morning of the trip arrived bright and sunny, filled with the sweet scent of blooming flowers and salt-tinged air. After piling into Anna's sleek SUV, we drove along the coast, windows down, music blasting, the ocean stretching out endlessly beside us. I glanced at Elliott beside me, his hand warmly entwined with mine, and felt my heart swell.

Anna's beach house was breathtaking—a sprawling, two-storey villa with floor-to-ceiling windows, pristine white walls, and a spacious veranda overlooking the sea. The turquoise waves crashed gently against the shoreline, inviting us to unwind completely.

We quickly settled in, throwing our bags into luxurious rooms before rushing toward the private stretch of sand. Anna, effortlessly charismatic, led the charge, her popularity something that always made me uneasy yet grateful to be close to her.

The day passed in a joyous blur—swimming, laughing, soaking in the sun. Elliott chased me across the sand, his playful teasing leaving my heart racing with happiness. For a moment, life felt uncomplicated, free from gossip, judgement, or fear. Just friends, sunshine, and love.

After sunset, we gathered around the poolside patio,

illuminated by strings of warm fairy lights. Anna, always the hostess, suggested we play games. "Let's do 'Never Have I Ever,'" she proposed, grinning mischievously.

We sat in a loose circle, cold drinks in hand, the night filled with laughter as we took playful jabs at each other's past mistakes and silly experiences. Anna was particularly animated, expertly balancing humour with gentle teasing.

"Never have I ever skipped class to go swimming," Elle declared boldly.

"Oh, come on!" Kayla laughed, raising her glass.

"You too?" Elliott feigned shock, winking at me. "I expected better from you!"

I giggled, nudging him playfully. "You're one to talk!"

"Never have I ever eaten an entire large pizza by myself," Kayla said, smirking.

Elliott rolled his eyes dramatically, lifting his glass. "Hey, it was one time!"

"Sure, Elliott," Anna teased. "And that was last weekend!"

We all laughed, our joy infectious and genuine. As the game continued, I felt completely at ease, until Anna leaned forward with a smirk. "Okay, my turn. Never have I ever kissed a girl."

My breath stilled momentarily, eyes darting quickly to Elle and Kayla. Elle had always known, and Kayla recently learned about Nic. Anna, however, was completely unaware.

Slowly, I raised my glass to my lips, feeling the eyes of my friends watching me closely.

Anna's eyes widened in surprise. "Seriously, Jasmine? Care to elaborate?"

I swallowed nervously, heart pounding. "There was someone," I began, voice hesitant, "but we kept it hidden because it wasn't exactly accepted... here."

Understanding flickered in Anna's expression. "It was Nic, wasn't it?"

I nodded slowly, glancing at Elliott, whose supportive smile encouraged me to continue. "It was beautiful but complicated. Elle always knew, and Kayla recently found out, but I wasn't ready to share it openly."

Kayla placed her hand gently on mine. "We always suspected, but we wanted you to tell us when you were ready."

Elle gave a supportive nod. "You don't owe anyone explanations. But we're here for you."

Anna smiled warmly after a brief pause. "We love you, Jasmine. All of you."

Emotion surged within me, relief mingled with gratitude. Elliott squeezed my hand reassuringly, silently echoing Anna's words.

Late that night, Elliott and I walked barefoot along the beach. The waves softly whispered along the shoreline, but Elliott's usually relaxed posture seemed tense, his gaze distant, distracted by thoughts I couldn't yet see.

"What's on your mind, Elliott?" I asked softly, gently touching his arm. "You've seemed distant tonight."

He paused, staring out at the moonlit ocean before finally turning to face me, vulnerability heavy in his eyes. "I've been meaning to tell you something. My parents—they're getting divorced. My mum wants to move back to the city."

Shock rippled through me, followed quickly by sadness. I could sense how deeply this weighed on him, his usual confidence fractured by uncertainty. "I'm so sorry, Elliott. That's a lot to process."

He nodded solemnly, voice thick with emotion. "I don't know exactly what it means for us yet. But it's been tearing me up inside, trying to figure out how to tell you."

I reached out, gently cupping his face to meet his eyes. "Whatever happens, Elliott, we'll navigate it together. Let's focus on enjoying every moment we have right now."

A faint smile touched his lips, his shoulders relaxing slightly. He pulled me into his embrace, holding me tightly beneath the star-filled sky. In the quiet strength of that moment, we silently promised each other to cherish every second, despite the uncertain future that lay ahead.

CHAPTER 7

Summer Promises

As each day passed, the exhilarating prospect of summer stretched ahead of us, filled with endless possibilities. Elliott and I had weathered the storm of rumours, confrontations, and lingering questions about my past. But beneath the excitement of carefree summer days, the uncertainty surrounding Elliott's possible move to the city hung over us like an invisible cloud. Still, we both silently decided to embrace every moment, cherishing the time we had together.

Our days became a tapestry of adventures woven with laughter, beach trips, and spontaneous drives across the island. We attended vibrant summer festivals, losing ourselves in the pulsing rhythms of reggae music, feasting on street food, and dancing barefoot beneath strings of colourful lights. Elliott and I even discovered a hidden waterfall, where we'd sneak away on scorching afternoons, laughing as we jumped into the cool, emerald pools beneath cascading waters.

Yet, despite the blissful days, I often noticed Elliott lost in thought, quietly troubled by his parents' recent separation. There were moments when his laughter would falter, and a shadow would pass over his usually bright eyes, reminding me that beneath our happiness was an undercurrent of uncertainty.

One sunny Saturday, my friends and I decided to take a girls' day trip to a quaint riverside restaurant nestled in lush greenery, known for its delicious seafood and serene ambience. Anna drove, of course, her bright yellow Jeep packed with snacks, music, and endless chatter.

As we arrived and settled at a rustic wooden table by the gently flowing river, Elle immediately grabbed the menu, excitedly scanning it with exaggerated enthusiasm.

"All right, ladies," Elle declared dramatically, "this is officially a no-drama zone today. Only good vibes and good food."

Kayla adjusted her wide-brimmed sun hat, rolling her eyes affectionately. "Elle, you say that like you aren't usually the source of the drama."

Elle pretended to gasp in mock offence, holding her hand over her heart. "I am offended. I'll have you know my life is a very peaceful place."

Anna smirked knowingly. "Sure, Elle. And I'm secretly an undercover spy."

We burst into laughter, the warmth and ease of friendship comforting my restless thoughts. Yet, despite the cheerful banter, Anna soon noticed my silence and leaned forward, her eyes gentle yet probing.

"Jas, what's really going on? You're quieter than usual."

I hesitated, feeling my friends' eyes on me, their concern palpable. Finally, I sighed, deciding to trust them with my worries. "It's Elliott. I know he's struggling with his parents' divorce. He tries to act like he's fine, but I can see he's really hurting."

Anna nodded thoughtfully. "That must be tough on him. Has he talked about it much?"

I shook my head gently. "He tries to keep it bottled up, but sometimes he just seems so lost. I wish there was something more I could do."

Elle offered a warm, reassuring smile. "Jasmine, just being there for him is already enough. You're his rock, even if he doesn't say it outright."

"Exactly," Kayla added, nodding. "You're doing everything you can. Elliott knows he's not alone because you're by his side."

Anna, always practical yet optimistic, chimed in with a comforting voice, "Maybe encourage him to talk more openly. Guys aren't always the best at sharing feelings, but Elliott clearly trusts you. Remind him you're there."

Their words filled me with a renewed sense of strength and determination. As our lunch continued, filled with laughter and playful teasing, I felt grateful for these friendships, each of them bringing something unique to our bond—Elle's infectious positivity, Kayla's quiet wisdom, and Anna's unwavering honesty.

Later that afternoon, I found myself back on Elliott's veranda, the faint sounds of music and bottles clinking from a nearby shop creating a familiar backdrop. Elliott's expression was contemplative, his gaze distant as he watched the sunset paint streaks of orange and purple across the sky.

"Elliott," I ventured softly, reaching for his hand. "It's okay to talk about it, you know. You don't have to carry everything alone."

He exhaled slowly, turning to me with vulnerability in his eyes. "I just feel torn. I love my parents, but this divorce... it feels like I'm losing parts of myself. My mum wants to move back to the city, and my dad wants to stay here. I'm stuck in the middle."

"I can't imagine how difficult that must be," I whispered gently. "But maybe there's a way to make things easier, at least for now."

He raised an eyebrow, a faint smile tugging at his lips. "You have an idea?"

"What if you stay here with your dad?" I proposed carefully. "Just until we finish sixth form. Then we could go to university in the city together next year. It could be the compromise your parents need to see."

His eyes widened slightly, hope sparking in them for the first time in days. "You think they'd go for that?"

I shrugged confidently. "We'll never know unless we try.

Plus, you've got me—writer extraordinaire—to help you craft the perfect pitch."

He chuckled warmly, nodding. "Okay, Miss Writer. Let's do it."

We spent the rest of the evening carefully crafting Elliott's plea, blending seriousness with just the right amount of heartfelt sincerity. When he finally made the call later that night, I waited anxiously, my phone clutched tightly in anticipation.

The moment my phone buzzed, my heart raced. "Elliott?"

"They agreed," he said, relief flooding his voice. "They actually said yes."

Joy surged through me, and I could hear the relief mirrored in his laugh. "Elliott, that's amazing! I knew they'd listen."

"It's all because of you," he said softly. "Thank you for everything."

"Always," I promised sincerely. "You're not alone in this. Never forget that."

The following days were filled with renewed excitement as we celebrated Elliott's news. Anna organised a bonfire at the beach, and we spent the night laughing beneath the stars, toasting marshmallows and making hopeful plans for our final school year together.

As the firelight danced across Elliott's face, illuminating his gentle smile, I felt a deep sense of peace. Despite the uncertainties ahead, we had each other, and that was more than enough.

"You've really changed me, Jasmine," Elliott whispered, pulling me closer as our friends' laughter filled the night air. "You've made me braver."

I smiled warmly, meeting his eyes. "We've made each other braver. No matter what happens, we'll face it together."

He leaned down, brushing his lips softly against mine, the kiss filled with promise, warmth, and unspoken reassurance. Beneath the stars, in the comforting glow of friendship and love, I knew our journey was only just beginning.

CHAPTER 8

Into the Light

Summer slipped by quickly, each day blurring into the next—filled with laughter, sunshine, and memories with Elliott and our friends. Slowly, I found myself stepping away from the shadows of my past, focusing instead on the exciting uncertainty that lay ahead. With the new school year approaching and our final year of sixth form around the corner, anticipation buzzed through me.

Yet, there was a nervous excitement stirring within me for other reasons. We'd all agreed that after sixth form, we would move to the city together for university—a thrilling yet intimidating prospect. I'd grown up in our small rural town, where everybody knew everyone, and going to the bustling city meant stepping far beyond my comfort zone. But knowing Elliott, Elle, Anna, and Kayla would be by my side calmed my fears. Together, we could face anything.

Summer had transformed us in more ways than one. Elliott and I had navigated difficult truths, while our group had grown stronger. Elliott, still coming to terms with the complexities of his parents' separation, showed admirable resilience. Our time together helped him find strength, and our friends were endlessly supportive, creating a solid foundation beneath us.

One evening, Elle burst into my room, practically glowing with excitement.

"Guys, there's an art showcase happening in town next weekend! Young artists, musicians, and poets—it's gonna be amazing," she announced dramatically, flopping onto my bed.

Anna raised an eyebrow from her spot at my vanity mirror, carefully applying eyeliner. "Since when do you care about poetry and art?"

Elle shrugged dramatically. "I don't, but it's a great reason to dress up and take pictures. Plus, Jasmine might actually enjoy it."

Kayla laughed softly from her corner, sketchbook in hand. "Elle, always the influencer."

"It sounds fun," I said thoughtfully. "Maybe we should go."

Anna raised an eyebrow, feigning surprise. "Jasmine wants to go out voluntarily? Who are you and what have you done with our shy friend?"

I laughed, feeling a sense of warmth at their easy banter. "Maybe I'm turning over a new leaf. You never know."

The weekend arrived quickly, bringing with it a rush of nerves. The showcase was held at a vibrant, eclectic venue filled with colourful murals, strung fairy lights, and soft, atmospheric music. Young people filled the space, their energy buzzing with creativity and excitement.

My heart raced as I signed up for the open mic segment, my fingers trembling slightly as I wrote my name. This was a huge step—a leap into vulnerability I'd never taken before.

"Are you sure about this?" Elliott whispered, his brown eyes filled with warmth and gentle concern.

I nodded, gripping his hand tightly. "I have to do this. It feels right."

Elle grinned, leaning in with enthusiasm. "Go up there and own it, Jasmine! You've got this."

As my name was called, my breath hitched. Stepping onto the stage, I felt the warmth of the spotlight bathe me, momentarily blinding as my heart raced. Standing before the microphone, my pulse quickened with nervous exhilaration.

Taking a steadying breath, I began:

Hidden truths beneath the surface,
Locked away in quiet fear,
Yet love blooms brave, defiant,
With whispers only hearts can hear.

Judged by shadows,
Weighed by silence,

Bound by rules I didn't choose,
But now I stand beneath these lights,
Ready to reclaim my truths.

My heart once hidden,
Love concealed,
I loved freely in the dark,
Gender fading, just a person—
Loving souls, not labels marked.

Now I step into the open,
Chains of secrecy undone,
My heart, my past, my journey,
Defined by me and me alone.

The applause erupted instantly—overwhelming and sincere. I felt tears prickling the corners of my eyes as relief surged through me. Elliott beamed proudly, and my friends cheered loudly, Elle even whooping enthusiastically. But as my gaze swept the crowd, my heart stopped.

Nic stood at the back, her expression unreadable.

Afterwards, as the buzz of conversation filled the room, Nic approached cautiously. My heart skipped—apprehensive, yet oddly calm.

"Hey," she said quietly, vulnerability evident in her eyes.

"Hi," I replied softly, nerves fluttering.

She took a deep breath. "That poem... it was beautiful. I wish I'd had that kind of courage back when we were together."

I hesitated, studying her. "It wasn't easy. Honestly, it took everything I had."

Nic's expression turned somber, thoughtful. "I'm glad you did it. Maybe it was time for both of us to move forward."

"Yeah," I agreed softly. "Maybe it was."

"I know I was harsh before," Nic said quietly, her voice strained. "But you deserve to live openly, however you choose. I hope you know that."

"Thank you," I replied, feeling genuinely grateful for her words. With a small nod, Nic melted back into the crowd, leaving me with a sense of finality and clarity I'd longed for.

That night, lying awake in my room, I found myself reflecting deeply on the past months. Once, I'd hidden behind insecurities—my writing tucked away in journals, my truths buried beneath layers of fear. I'd felt unsure about my dark chocolate skin, worried about how the world saw me, scared of judgment and rejection.

But tonight, as the moonlight gently illuminated my room, I realized I was no longer the same Jasmine. I had evolved. The girl who once feared her own reflection was now embracing every aspect of herself. My heart swelled with pride and newfound confidence.

I was no longer defined by the shadows of my past or the fears that once held me back.

I was stepping into the light—bold, unafraid, and ready to embrace everything the future had to offer.

CHAPTER 9

New Beginnings, New Hurdles

The first day back at school was always buzzing with renewed energy and fresh starts, but this year felt especially charged. Our final year of sixth form had officially begun, and with university looming on the horizon, everything seemed to hold greater significance. I walked through the familiar hallways alongside Elliott, Elle, Anna, and Kayla, comforted by the sense of normalcy their presence provided.

As we chatted animatedly about our schedules, Anna suddenly paused mid-sentence, glancing toward the entrance with surprise lighting her face.

"Oh! She actually came," Anna gasped, eyes sparkling. We all followed her gaze to a striking girl strolling confidently toward us—her honey-toned skin glowing, long, silky hair cascading perfectly down her back. She was the kind of effortlessly beautiful girl who commanded attention without even trying.

"Who's that?" Elle asked, immediately intrigued.

"That's my cousin from Kingston," Anna explained excitedly. "Her name's Bianca. Her parents moved abroad for a year, so she's staying with us."

"She looks like she stepped right off Instagram," Kayla murmured in awe.

"Hey, Anna," Bianca greeted warmly, flashing a dazzling smile that revealed perfect white teeth. Her gaze drifted to the rest of us, pausing noticeably on Elliott. Her eyes sparkled with interest, lingering a beat too long.

I felt a tightness form in my chest—an unfamiliar pang of insecurity.

"Bianca, these are my friends—Elle, Kayla, Jasmine, and Elliott," Anna introduced cheerfully.

Bianca's smile deepened as she studied Elliott. "Nice to meet you all. Especially you," she directed smoothly at Elliott, her voice dripping with confidence.

Elliott glanced at me briefly, clearly sensing the sudden shift in mood. "Nice to meet you too," he replied politely, wrapping an arm around my waist to reassure me silently. It helped—a little.

Throughout the day, Bianca became an instant sensation. Stories of her life in the city, travels to Europe and Asia, and extravagant adventures filled every conversation. Boys were charmed by her stories, and girls seemed desperate for her approval. It felt as if the entire sixth form was enchanted by her presence.

Yet something about her left me uneasy. Maybe it was the slight smirk she wore when she noticed me watching, or perhaps it was the subtle way she inserted herself into conversations near Elliott. Whatever it was, it nagged at me relentlessly.

That afternoon, Elliott and I sat beneath our favourite tree during lunch. He squeezed my hand gently, sensing my turmoil.

"You know you've got nothing to worry about, right?" he reassured softly.

I sighed, resting my head against his shoulder. "I know. It's just... she seems so perfect, Elliott. Everyone loves her."

"Not everyone," he whispered, brushing his thumb gently over my hand. "You see past her surface, Jasmine. Trust your instincts."

Days turned into weeks, and Bianca's presence became impossible to ignore. It seemed wherever Elliott went, Bianca would somehow find a reason to be nearby. Anna, blind to her cousin's manoeuvres, delightedly encouraged their interactions, thrilled to have family fitting into her circle.

One evening, as we all hung out at Anna's house, Bianca cornered me in the kitchen. "Must be tiring, always worrying he'll realise you're not enough," she whispered, smiling coldly.

I felt a rush of anger and hurt, but I refused to give her the satisfaction. "You don't scare me, Bianca. Elliott and I are solid."

She laughed softly, tossing her hair over her shoulder. "We'll see."

The tension simmered beneath the surface of our friend group, unnoticed by all except Elliott, who remained steadfastly by my side. Still, I couldn't shake the creeping anxiety. Bianca seemed determined to chip away at my confidence.

Late one night, Elliott found me sitting on my verandah, staring into the darkness. He sat quietly beside me, his presence comforting.

"I see what's happening, Jasmine," he murmured gently. "I'm not blind. But no matter what Bianca says or does, she can't change how I feel about you."

I met his eyes—vulnerable yet hopeful. "Promise?"

"I promise," he whispered firmly, sealing it with a tender kiss.

Yet, even as I leaned into his reassurance, I knew deep down this battle had just begun—and Bianca wasn't the type to back down without a fight.

The weeks continued, and Bianca's influence spread through the school like wildfire. It seemed like each day she invented new ways to subtly undermine my relationship. She charmed Elliott's friends with lavish stories and invited them to exclusive parties at Anna's house, making me feel increasingly isolated.

One particularly difficult day, Kayla noticed my quiet distress at our usual lunchtime spot by the poinciana tree.

"Jasmine, you okay? You've been quiet lately."

I sighed deeply, finally opening up about everything—the whispered comments, Bianca's thinly veiled insults, and my growing insecurities. Kayla listened patiently, her eyes soft with empathy.

"Jasmine, Bianca may have everyone else fooled, but we know who you are. You're real, authentic, and kind. Elliott loves you for exactly who you are, and nothing she does can change that."

Elle jumped in with her usual humour, "Honestly, Jasmine, Bianca's just jealous. She might have travelled the world, but she'll never have your heart, your beauty, or your incredible poetry skills."

Anna nodded, suddenly serious. "You're stronger than she is, Jasmine. Don't ever doubt yourself."

Their words wrapped around me like a protective cloak, fortifying my resolve. I smiled, grateful beyond words for their unwavering support. I felt a renewed sense of confidence.

Bianca might be determined, but so was I.
And now, more than ever, I was ready to fight for the life and love I had built.

CHAPTER 10

Unveiled Truths

The morning breeze carried an unusual chill as I stepped through the school gates, signalling that something was undeniably wrong. Sixth form had always been filled with whispers and drama, but today, the stares felt pointed—conversations quieted as I walked past. Anxiety twisted my stomach into knots.

"Hey, Jasmine," Elle greeted softly, pulling me aside. Her typically bright eyes were clouded with genuine worry. "Have you seen what's been posted?"

"What now?" I asked, bracing myself.

Elle hesitated before handing me her phone. My heart sank as my eyes fell on the school's gossip page. There it was —a grainy photo of Nic and me from the poetry event, taken at just the wrong angle. My stomach twisted painfully as I read the cruel caption: "Jasmine's relationship with

Elliott is fake. Guess she forgot to tell him her secret. Nic knows the truth."

Heat rushed to my face. Anger boiled beneath the embarrassment, but fear was strongest. Bianca's smug face flashed in my mind immediately. This had her name written all over it.

Elle gently squeezed my shoulder, bringing me back. "Are you okay?"

I forced a shaky smile. "I'll survive."

But inside, my heart raced wildly, each beat echoing the whispers around me.

The day dragged on painfully. My literature class usually calmed me, but today I struggled to pay attention. Across the room, Kayla shot sympathetic glances my way, her eyes filled with concern. When lunchtime arrived, I was desperate to find peace under the fiery branches of the large poinciana tree—our favourite refuge.

Elle approached cautiously, biting her lip as she sat beside me. "Jas, I didn't want to stress you more in class, but Bianca was really going all out today in chemistry."

I sighed deeply. "What exactly happened?"

Elle rolled her eyes dramatically. "She practically threw herself at Elliott, laughing too loudly at his jokes, leaning into him at every chance. Even Mr. Harris noticed and had to separate their lab tables. Elliott tried ignoring her, though —he looked really uncomfortable."

My chest tightened. "Did he see the post?"

Elle nodded slowly. "Yeah, he did. He seemed tense after

class. I could tell it bothered him."

A sickening dread settled in me. Despite knowing Elliott, uncertainty gnawed at the edges of my trust. The rest of the school day blurred painfully, my mind looping anxiously until Elliott and I met after school on his verandah.

The late-afternoon air felt heavy. Nearby, laughter and the distant sound of bottles clinking formed an ironic backdrop. Elliott's dark eyes avoided mine, filled with discomfort and uncertainty.

"Jasmine," he finally broke the silence, his voice strained, "about the post…"

I braced myself, hurt already pooling in my chest. "You believed it?"

His eyes widened. "No—not exactly. But it caught me off guard. Bianca kept whispering about it throughout chemistry class, saying things to make me question everything."

Tears stung behind my eyes, my voice shaking. "So you doubted me."

He flinched, guilt clouding his expression. "Jasmine, I'm sorry. I should've known better."

A heavy silence hung between us.

"I've always been honest with you, Elliott."

"I know," he whispered, desperation edging his voice as he reached toward me. But I stepped back instinctively, the betrayal sharp.

"Jasmine, please—"

"No. I think we both need space," I said softly, turning

away before he could see the tears spilling down my cheeks.

I walked away from the one person who had always made me feel safe, my heart splintering with each step.

That afternoon, my emotions drove me to my quiet spot near another poinciana tree by the river. Its fiery petals danced gently in the wind, an ironic beauty compared to my turmoil.

"Jasmine?"

Startled, I turned to see Nic approaching cautiously, hands buried deep in her pockets. "Can I sit?"

I hesitated but nodded. "Sure."

"I saw the post," Nic began, eyes fixed on the tree. "I just needed you to know I had nothing to do with it."

"I know," I replied softly. "It was Bianca."

Nic exhaled deeply. "She reached out to me, too—fishing for dirt. I ignored her. But it made me realise something."

"What?" I asked carefully.

"You always had courage I admired. Seeing you openly happy with Elliott hurt, and maybe part of me resented you for being brave enough to move on. But I never wanted you to get hurt like this."

Her honesty was raw, genuine, and disarming.

"Thank you, Nic. That means a lot."

Nic smiled gently, sincere. "Let me help you clear your name. Bianca sent me something by mistake that proves everything."

The evidence Nic provided was damning—an accidental text clearly exposing Bianca's malicious scheme. Fury replaced my fear, determination burning fiercely within me.

I decided to confront Bianca the next morning. The sixth form lounge was full, buzzing with morning conversations as I approached Bianca confidently, head high despite my racing heart.

"Bianca," my voice was steady, calm. "Did you really think spreading lies about me would get you Elliott?"

Bianca scoffed arrogantly, her glossy lips twisting into a cruel smile. "Truth hurts, Jasmine. You can't hide who you are forever."

I held up my phone, displaying the screenshot Nic had given me. Bianca's eyes widened in shock as whispers erupted around us.

"Pathetic," I said quietly. "You almost ruined something good because of jealousy."

Anna stepped forward, anger shaking her usually calm demeanour. "You're my cousin, Bianca. But this is beyond disgusting."

Bianca turned red, her eyes blazing angrily as she stormed away—humiliated—leaving awkward silence behind her.

Later that afternoon, Elliott found me beneath our poinciana tree, eyes heavy with remorse. "Jasmine, I'm so sorry. You deserved better than my doubts."

His vulnerability pierced through my lingering hurt. "It felt terrible knowing you questioned me."

He nodded, regret shadowing his expression. "I'll never make that mistake again. Trusting you is the easiest thing I've ever done. Forgive me?"

I squeezed his hand, warmth flooding back into my heart. "Already forgiven."

That evening, Nic and I shared a final conversation beneath the warm glow of streetlights. We exchanged heartfelt apologies, healing past wounds and freeing ourselves from the bitterness that had haunted us for too long.

Walking home afterward, I felt lighter, a weight finally lifted. A true confidence grew stronger in my chest, shaped by the experiences that tested me and the people who stood by my side.

Later, my friends gathered in my room, comforting and supportive. Elle dramatically recounted the confrontation in vivid detail, making us laugh despite ourselves.

"I thought Bianca's eyes might actually pop out," Elle exclaimed, imitating Bianca's shocked face.

Anna groaned in embarrassment. "Honestly, I'm sorry I didn't realise how manipulative she was earlier."

Kayla, sketching quietly in her notebook, smiled mischievously. "Next art project: Bianca's meltdown. I'll call it Entitlement Collapsing."

Their laughter filled my room, a balm soothing the residual sting of betrayal. As their voices filled the night, warmth enveloped me. Friendships that had deepened, healed, and strengthened felt stronger than ever.

That night, alone in bed, I reflected on everything I'd overcome. For so long, insecurity had held me back—about my chocolate-brown skin, about my writing, my identity.

But now I stood in the truth of who I was: confident, brave, unapologetically myself.

I smiled softly to myself, feeling calm certainty wash over me.

No matter what challenges lay ahead, I knew who I was—and I was ready to embrace whatever came next.

The past had shaped me, but it would no longer define me.

My future belonged to me alone.

CHAPTER 11

Finding Balance

The stress of the past few weeks had left me feeling drained. Between the chaos stirred by Bianca, the relentless whispers in the hallways, and mending my relationship with Elliott, it seemed my life was spinning out of control. The biggest casualty, however, was something far more critical: my academics.

Each day at school became a test of endurance, each assignment harder than the last. My concentration waned, words blurring on the pages of my textbooks. Tests I once breezed through now felt overwhelming. Panic crept in every time I thought about my dream of studying literature at university, where admission relied heavily on grades. The pressure was intensified by the looming scholarship deadline. Without it, I knew university tuition would be a huge burden on my family.

At home, life continued at its usual steady pace, unaware of the storm brewing within me. My family's routine had always provided me with comfort. Our house, modest but warm, was a small haven tucked at the end of a quiet street. The walls held years of laughter, secrets shared, and endless support. But now, each step through the front door brought pangs of guilt and worry.

My father, always gentle and soft-spoken, was usually the first face I saw when I returned from school. His presence was like a warm embrace—comforting, reassuring. He'd sit quietly in his favourite chair, reading his latest novel or preparing notes for a case. His glasses perched gently on his nose, his expression calm even in stressful times.

My mother was his opposite—strong-willed and vocal, a natural leader whose passion filled every room she entered. She managed to be both nurturing and assertive, always finding balance in her love. Her position at the local bank made her efficient and practical, qualities that spilled over into her parenting.

Then there was my ten-year-old sister, Zoe—spirited, vibrant, and talented. Zoe was a whirlwind of energy, excelling effortlessly at everything she tried, from academics and sports to music. Even at ten, her accomplishments overshadowed mine at times. Still, I adored her infectious laughter and endless optimism.

One evening, I sat at our kitchen table, textbooks sprawled across its surface. Zoe, finishing homework effortlessly, hummed softly while our parents chatted quietly nearby. I stared blankly at the pages, words swimming as frustration mounted.

"Jasmine, are you okay?" my father's gentle voice broke through my thoughts. He'd noticed my distress before I could hide it.

"Yeah, Dad. I'm fine," I said, forcing a smile that felt painfully fake.

He set his papers down, meeting my eyes softly. "Are you sure, sweetheart? You've seemed distracted lately."

I opened my mouth to reassure him, but my mother's sharp eyes caught mine, understanding flickering across her face. She nodded gently at me, silently promising we'd talk later.

"Maybe just tired," I admitted quietly, hoping it was enough.

Dad nodded, sensing the fragility of my mood. "Alright. Just remember, we're always here."

Later that night, as I sat on my bed staring hopelessly at my half-completed sociology essay, a soft knock interrupted me.

"Can I come in?" Mom asked gently from the doorway, her eyes filled with concern.

"Yeah," I sighed, pushing aside my notes.
She closed the door softly, sitting beside me. Her presence immediately calmed my frayed nerves.

"Sweetheart, your grades have dropped," she began gently, her voice calm yet direct. "Your sociology teacher called today. She's worried. I'm worried, Jasmine."

My chest tightened. "I'm sorry, Mom. It's just... things have been tough lately."

She brushed the hair softly from my face, her eyes sympathetic. "I know, love. With Bianca and the gossip—it's understandable you're struggling. But remember your goals, Jasmine. You've worked too hard to let someone else derail your dreams."

My eyes burned with tears. "I feel like I'm losing control, mom. Everything's overwhelming, and I don't know how to fix it."

She sighed softly, pulling me into a comforting embrace. "Honey, listen. You're strong. You always have been. I know it's difficult, but you can't let your circumstances define you. You're the same Jasmine who stood on stage bravely sharing your poetry. Don't lose sight of her."

I clung to her words, comforted by her unwavering faith. "I'm scared I might not qualify for the scholarship. If my grades keep dropping, university might not be possible."

She gently cupped my face. "Jasmine, look at me. Your father and I have always been proud of you—not just your accomplishments, but who you are. This scholarship would help, yes, but your worth doesn't hinge on it."

A quiet sob escaped me, vulnerability spilling freely. "I just want to make you proud."

"Oh, Jasmine." Her voice was thick with emotion, eyes glistening. "You already have, more than you'll ever know. Remember when you told us about Nic? How you faced it bravely, despite being afraid? Your father and I admired your strength, your truth. Nothing could ever change how proud we are of you."

I took a deep breath, relief washing over me. "Thank you, mom. I needed to hear that."

"Always," she said firmly, pressing a soft kiss to my forehead. "Now, rest. Tomorrow, we'll tackle this together —one step at a time."

I nodded, feeling a sense of determination reawaken within me.

The next morning, I woke to Zoe's bright eyes peeking curiously into my room. "Morning, Jaz! Feeling better?"

I laughed softly, pulling my spirited little sister into a hug. "Much better, thanks to mom."

Zoe grinned brightly, eyes sparkling. "Good, because you promised to help me with my science project today. I already know exactly what I want to do."

"Let me guess—another complicated masterpiece?" I teased, earning a playful jab.

Throughout the morning, helping Zoe, I felt grounded. Her endless enthusiasm was contagious, and her chatter helped push away my lingering anxiety.

"You know," Zoe said thoughtfully, "Mom and Dad always say how proud they are of you. I hope I make them proud, too."

I paused, touched by her innocent confession. "Zoe, they're already proud of you. Trust me."

She smiled warmly, hugging me tightly. "And I'm proud of you too, Jaz."

I blinked back tears, holding her close. "Thank you, Zoe. You have no idea how much that means."

Back at school, renewed determination guided my steps. I took extra notes in class, stayed late at the library, and even agreed to tutoring sessions with Kayla and Elle. Elliott also helped, patiently explaining complex concepts during our quiet study sessions on his verandah.

Gradually, the fog of stress cleared. My confidence returned with each assignment completed, every test passed. My grades began to stabilise again, and I even found time to work on my scholarship application.

One evening, as Elliott and I studied together, he reached over and squeezed my hand gently. "You seem happier lately, Jas. Lighter."

I smiled softly, meeting his warm gaze. "I feel lighter. My mom reminded me who I am and why my dreams matter."

Elliott's eyes filled with warmth. "I'm glad. I've missed seeing you like this."

I leaned into him, grateful for his support. "Thanks for standing by me, Elliott. Even when things got rough."

He kissed the top of my head softly. "Always, Jasmine."

As weeks passed, my family became my steady foundation once again. Evening dinners were filled with laughter and playful banter, my parents exchanging loving glances, Zoe sharing stories of her day. Home felt safe again.

One quiet evening, as we cleared the dinner dishes, my father placed a reassuring hand on my shoulder, his voice gentle. "We're proud of you, Jasmine. No matter what happens."

Mom smiled warmly, nodding in agreement. Zoe beamed brightly, giving me a thumbs-up.

I smiled, warmth flooding through me. "I know. And that means everything."

As I retreated to my room, confidence filled my chest. The storm had passed. Though uncertainties remained, I had reclaimed my balance, supported by the unwavering love of my family.

I was ready again—determined, focused, and stronger. And whatever lay ahead, I knew I'd face it with courage.

Chapter 12

The Final Test

The highlighter in my hand hovered over the page, but this time, it was not panic that clouded my focus—it was determination. The weight of final exams loomed, yes, but I was no longer unraveling under pressure. My desk was still cluttered with sticky notes, past papers, and textbooks, but I had reclaimed my balance.

The girl sitting at this desk was different now—more grounded, more self-assured. I knew what was at stake. To get into the Humanities programme at university, I needed top grades. More than that, I needed the scholarship. My parents never made me feel the burden of our finances, but I understood it all the same.

But I also understood something else: I was capable.

I reviewed my schedule one subject at a time, breaking each syllabus down into manageable parts. Literature in the morning, Sociology after lunch, revision quizzes with Kayla and Elle in the evenings. I timed my breaks, stayed hydrated, and journaled whenever the anxiety whispered too loudly.

There were still moments when uncertainty tried to creep in. The nights were especially hard—quiet and echoing with doubts—but I met those feelings with grace. I reminded myself that I was prepared, that I was no longer running from the version of myself who once felt small.

One afternoon, as I highlighted a passage from *The Tempest*, my phone buzzed with a message from Elle.

Elle: Still alive?

Kayla: If you don't answer, I'm assuming you drowned in textbooks.

Me: Barely hanging on.

Elle: We're kidnapping you tomorrow. Non-negotiable.

I laughed softly. My friends always knew when to step in.

The next day, Elle linked arms with me before Biology class, her face unusually serious.

"Jas, you need to hear this," she whispered.

"What now?" I asked, already bracing myself.

She sighed. "I overheard Bianca in class. She told her friends you're only with Elliott because you needed a rebound after Nic. That you chose a 'safe option' now that you're done experimenting."

My body went still. The insult landed—but it did not shake me.

"That's disgusting," I said, my voice calm.

Elle's eyes flashed. "It took everything in me not to say something."

I nodded, a quiet resolve settling in. "She's trying to get in my head. But she's too late."

And I meant it.

That night, I returned to my desk, and this time, the words in my literature textbook did not blur. They sharpened. I reviewed key themes, scribbled essay outlines, and jotted down memorable quotes. I sipped tea, flipped through flashcards, and even read aloud to strengthen my focus.

I was not perfect. But I was prepared.

The following weeks passed in a blur of revision sessions, early mornings, and quiet prayer. I studied beneath the blooming poinciana tree at school, in the quiet corners of the library, and at home with Zoe's music floating in from the next room. Elliott and I quizzed each other when we could. Kayla lent me her sociology notes, and Elle kept my spirits high with humour and perfectly timed memes.

When the first exam morning arrived, I stood outside the hall, breathing in the humid, rain-scented air. The sky was overcast, but I felt clear.

Inside, the invigilators paced the aisles, distributing exam papers with quiet efficiency. My hands were steady as I flipped mine over and read the first question.

How does adversity shape personal identity in literature?

A slow smile tugged at my lips.

I thought of everything—Bianca's games, Nic's betrayal, the rumours, the doubts. I thought of the girl I used to be, afraid to share her writing, unsure of her reflection. I thought of the Jasmine who had stepped into the spotlight, into her truth.

And then I wrote.

I poured myself into the pages. I made every sentence count.

That afternoon, I submitted my final scholarship application.

Stepping out of the school building, the warm breeze met my skin, soft and full of promise. It smelled like the edge of rain and beginnings.

Elle, Kayla, Anna, and Elliott were waiting near the gates.

" Well?" Elle grinned. "How'd it go?"

I exhaled, smiling. "I think... I did my best."

"That's all that matters," Elliott said, pulling me into a hug.

Kayla clapped me on the back. "Damn right it is. Now, can we please celebrate before my brain melts?"

I laughed, the sound light and real.

No matter what the results said, I knew I had shown up for myself. I had silenced the noise, focused on my dreams, and honoured my voice.

And that—that was enough.

For now, it was finally time to breathe.

CHAPTER 13

Letting Go

The morning sunlight poured through the windows of the school auditorium, illuminating the sea of students anxiously waiting for their final results. The air was thick with tension—the quiet rustling of paper and whispered conversations only amplifying the nerves hanging over all of us.

My palms were clammy as I stood with Elliott, Elle, Anna, and Kayla, my stomach tied in knots. Today was the day we would find out whether all the late nights, the stress, and the sacrifices had been worth it.

The headmistress, a stern but fair woman with hair always neatly combed into a perfect updo, stepped onto the stage and cleared her throat.

"Sixth formers, today marks the culmination of your hard work. We are proud of each and every one of you."

"Remember, your grades do not define you, but they are a stepping stone to the future you are building."

A wave of hushed anticipation spread across the room as the envelopes with our names were distributed. The weight of my entire academic career sat in my hands—a single sheet of paper separating me from my dreams.

I took a deep breath, swallowing hard before peeling it open.

Literatures in English: 1 (with distinction)
Sociology: 1 (with distinction)
Caribbean Studies: 1
Communication Studies: 1 (with distinction)

The world tilted for a moment as I stared at the results. I had done it. I had gotten everything I needed.

I turned, my hands trembling as I looked up at Elliott. His gaze met mine, a slow smile spreading across his face as he opened his own envelope.

"Well?" I asked, my voice barely above a whisper.

His grin widened. "I passed. All ones!"

I let out a breathless laugh, relief rushing through me. "Elliott, that's amazing!"

Elle tackled me from the side, practically bouncing with excitement. "Jasmine, you aced it! This is your moment!"

Anna and Kayla hugged me from both sides, the tension in my chest melting away as my friends celebrated alongside me.

But just as the relief settled in, another reality hit me.

The scholarship.

I had no idea if I had gotten it yet.

The thought sobered me as we all made our way outside. Elliott took my hand, pulling me aside from the excited chatter of our classmates. "Are you okay?"

I nodded, but my fingers curled tightly around the envelope. "I just... I need to know about the scholarship. It's the last piece of the puzzle."

He studied me, then sighed softly, squeezing my hand. "And if you get it?"

I blinked. "What do you mean?"

Elliott glanced toward the school gates, his expression contemplative. "If you get it, Jasmine, you might have to leave sooner. And if you don't... I just... I don't want this to change us."

My chest tightened. "Elliott, nothing is going to change us."

He exhaled sharply. "I know. But the future is happening so fast."

I reached up, cupping his cheek. "Whatever happens, we'll figure it out."

His lips quirked into a small, lopsided smile, the tension in his shoulders easing. "You always know what to say."

I kissed him gently, sealing the promise between us.

Later that evening, I got a text from Nic.

Nic: Hey, can we meet up? I have something I want to say before I leave.

I hesitated for a moment before typing:

Me: Sure. Smoothie spot?

A few hours later, I walked into the little smoothie shop tucked into the town square, the scent of fresh fruit and blended ice filling the air. Nic was already there, sitting at a corner table with her usual mango smoothie in hand.

She looked up as I approached, offering a small smile. "Hey."

"Hey," I said, sliding into the chair across from her.

For a moment, we just studied each other, the weight of our shared history lingering between us.

"I wanted to say congratulations," Nic said, stirring her drink with her straw. "I heard about your grades. I always knew you'd do amazing."

"Thank you," I said genuinely. "That means a lot."

Nic exhaled, running a hand through her short curls. "I'm leaving soon. Got into law school abroad."

A flicker of surprise passed through me. "That's amazing, Nic. I'm happy for you."

She smiled, but there was something wistful in her eyes. "It's weird, isn't it? How much has changed?"

I nodded. "Yeah. It is."

Nic took a deep breath. "I was angry for a long time. I thought you were choosing an easier path, but... I realize now that you were just choosing yourself. And that's not a bad thing."

Emotion swelled in my chest. "Nic..."

"I just wanted to say I'm sorry. For all of it," she said.

"And I hope you're happy, Jasmine. Really happy."

A lump formed in my throat, but I smiled. "I am. And I hope you are too."

She nodded, lifting her smoothie. "To fresh starts?"

I lifted mine in return. "To fresh starts."

As we parted ways for the last time, I felt lighter than I had in years.

The next morning, my phone buzzed with an email notification.

Subject: Scholarship Decision – University of the West Indies

My hands shook as I opened it, my heart hammering against my ribs.

Dear Miss Jasmine Sinclair,
We are pleased to inform you that you have been selected as the recipient of the Humanities Excellence Scholarship...

The words blurred together as tears welled in my eyes.

I had done it. I had actually done it.

I sprinted out of my room, nearly tripping over myself as I yelled, "Mum! Dad! I GOT IT!"

My mother emerged from the kitchen, wide-eyed, while my father lowered his newspaper.

"You got the scholarship?" my mother gasped.

I nodded frantically, tears spilling down my cheeks. "Yes!"

A wide smile broke across my father's face as he pulled

me into a hug. My mother quickly joined, squeezing me tightly. "We're so proud of you, sweetheart," my father murmured.

"You worked so hard for this," my mum added. "This is just the beginning."

Zoe peeked into the room, grinning. "So does this mean I get your room when you leave?"

We all burst into laughter, and for the first time in months, I felt completely, utterly at peace.

That evening, Elliott showed up at my house, holding a bouquet of my favourite flowers.

"I had to celebrate you properly," he said with a grin, handing them to me.

"Elliott," I breathed, taking them with a soft smile.

"Come on," he said, taking my hand. "I have something to tell you."

We drove to the same quiet spot where we had spent countless evenings watching the sunset. As we sat on the hood of his car, he turned to me, his expression serious but excited.

"I got into university," he said.

My eyes widened. "Elliott, that's amazing!"

He exhaled slowly, running a hand through his hair. "Not just any university, Jasmine. The same one as you."

I froze, my mind catching up to his words.

"You—what?"

"I applied a while back," he admitted, watching my reaction

carefully. "I didn't say anything because I didn't know if I'd get in."

Tears pricked at my eyes. "You mean… we're going to university together?"

He smiled, nodding. "Yeah. We are."

Without thinking, I threw my arms around him, my heart bursting with happiness.

"We're actually doing this," I whispered.

"We are," he murmured against my hair. "Together."

That night, as I stood on my veranda, taking in the quiet hum of the night, I thought about everything that had led me here.

Once, I had been afraid.

Afraid of being seen, of stepping into my light.

But now?

Now, I was ready.

For the city.

For university.

For this next chapter of my life.

And I couldn't wait to begin.

CHAPTER 14

The Beginning of Everything

The last day of school arrived faster than I expected. The halls that once felt suffocating now seemed full of memories—whispers of laughter, hushed conversations, the weight of insecurities I had carried for too long. I trailed my fingers along the cool metal of my locker, staring at the stickers and scribbled notes left behind over the years. I had walked these corridors as a girl unsure of herself, afraid to be seen. Now, I was walking out as someone entirely different.

"Can you believe this is it?" Elle asked, nudging me as we stood outside our classroom for the last time.

I smiled softly. "I really can't. It feels like we just started."

Kayla, who was sketching absentmindedly on the back of her notebook, looked up. "I'm still processing the fact that we won't be coming back here in September. It's weird."

Anna appeared, flicking her perfectly straightened hair

over her shoulder. "It's liberating, if you ask me," she said with a smirk. "No more uniforms, no more rules—just the real world waiting for us."

"That sounds a little terrifying," I admitted, adjusting my bag strap.

"Terrifying and exciting," Elliott chimed in, joining our circle with a grin. "We've spent so long dreaming about the future. Now, it's actually here."

The weight of his words settled over us. We weren't kids anymore. We were stepping into something bigger than ourselves.

We spent the rest of the day saying our goodbyes, leaving notes in each other's yearbooks, and reminiscing about inside jokes that once seemed like the biggest things in the world. As we exited the school gates for the final time, I turned back for one last look.

I wasn't the same girl who had walked into these halls all those years ago.

I was someone new.

The auditorium buzzed with nervous excitement as the graduation ceremony began. The headmistress gave her usual speech about perseverance, but it was the guest speaker who truly captured our attention.

A renowned Caribbean author stood on the stage, her presence commanding but warm.

"Your voice matters," she said, her eyes scanning the crowd. "Your stories, your experiences—no one can tell them the way you can. So take up space. Speak boldly. Be unafraid of who you are."

I felt her words in my chest.

I had spent so long hiding parts of myself, but now I understood—I was meant to take up space in this world. Elle, our valedictorian, took the stage next.

"Wow. I can't believe they actually trusted me to give this speech," she started, making the audience laugh. "But seriously—these past years have been filled with chaos, stress, and way too many late-night study sessions. But they've also been filled with love, friendship, and memories I wouldn't trade for anything."

She paused, her usual confidence softening. "We made it. And as we move forward, let's not just chase success. Let's chase happiness—in whatever form that takes."

The applause that followed was deafening.

After the ceremony, we took pictures in our caps and gowns, capturing the moment forever.

As we stood together, Anna sighed dramatically. "I am not ready for all the sappy goodbyes."

"Too bad," Kayla said, smirking. "We're doing them anyway."

Anna laughed, but her voice cracked slightly when she turned to us. "I'm gonna miss you guys."

Elle threw her arms around her. "We're not disappearing, dummy. We're just spreading out a little."

Anna was leaving for business school at a university overseas. Elle was heading to medical school, and Kayla was following her dreams of becoming an artist at the visual and performing arts school.

As I hugged Anna tightly outside the airport, it truly hit me.

"This isn't the end," I told her, swallowing the lump in my throat.

She blinked rapidly, forcing a smile. "No, it's not. But it is different."

"It is," I agreed. "But we'll make it work."

We squeezed each other's hands before she grabbed her suitcase and disappeared through the gates.

Standing there, surrounded by my friends and the life I was about to leave behind, I felt both excitement and fear battling in my chest.

I wasn't just stepping into a new chapter.

I was stepping into an entirely new life.

That night, Elliott and I took one last walk through town. The streets felt different, almost like they knew we were leaving soon.

He took my hand, his thumb tracing slow circles against my skin.

"We've come a long way, haven't we?" he mused.

I smiled softly. "Yeah, we have."

Elliott stopped walking, turning to face me fully. "No matter where life takes us, we've got this."

I knew he wasn't making a forever promise. He was making a right now promise. And that was enough.

The day I left for university, I stood on my veranda one last time, taking it all in.

The place where I had spent my childhood. The place where I had fallen in love. The place where I had discovered myself.

I wasn't scared anymore.

I had grown into the person I was always meant to be.

I looked out at the morning sun, letting the warmth settle into my skin, and breathed deeply.

My little sister ran onto the veranda, her laughter echoing. "Are you ready, Jazzy?"

I grinned. "Yeah, I am."

Elliott honked from the driveway, and I turned to see my friends piling into the car.

My mother stepped beside me, brushing a hand over my hair like she used to when I was little. "I'm so proud of you," she whispered.

My dad, a man of few words, embraced me tightly. Without him saying anything, I felt all his emotions. I felt their love. I would miss them.

I swallowed hard, giving them one last hug before grabbing my bags and heading to the car.

As the car pulled away, I watched my small hometown fade into the distance, and ahead of me, the city skyline grew larger.

A new adventure was waiting.

And this time—I was ready for it.

About the Author

KAYANNA J. WILLIAMS is an aspiring writer with a passion for crafting emotionally resonant stories and poems that explore the themes of love, identity, and personal growth. With a background in creative writing and various writing workshops, she has honed the skills to bring relatable characters to life. Although she has not yet published any work, she is always writing. Living as a young adult in Jamaica, Kayanna draws inspiration from her own journeys of love, friendship, and the experiences of those around her. In her free time, she enjoys reading various genres, exploring new places through writing, and being a supportive friend. She believes in capturing the essence of life's moments—both the joyful and the challenging—and expressing them through the written word.

www.ingramcontent.com/pod-product-compliance
Lightning Source LLC
Chambersburg PA
CBHW020652010826
48969CB00012B/824